Jim Henson's™

BEAR in the **BIG BLUE HOUSE**™

I LOVE BEAR

by Nancy Inteli
illustrated by Carolyn Bracken

Random House 🏠 New York

Based on the TV series *BEAR IN THE BIG BLUE HOUSE*™ created by Mitchell Kriegman.
Produced by The Jim Henson Company for Disney Channel.

Good morning, Ray!

Treelo brings Bear fresh berries.

Can you name the three types
of berries that Treelo brought?

Bear wants to make
triple-berry pancakes!

Tutter helps Bear make breakfast.

Mmm. These pancakes smell great!

Yum! Yum! Pip and Pop share their pancakes.

Circle the foods you like to eat for breakfast.

It's time to clean up.

Tutter cleans his mouse hole.

Now it's time for tea.

Connect the dots to see
who joins the party.

Wow! Pirate Pip and First Mate Pop have a treasure map.

Everyone goes to look for the hidden treasure!

Help the pirates find the treasure.

Ahoy! Ojo Orangebeard and Captain Treelo
find a treasure chest.

It's filled with clams!

Bear and his friends love to play games outside.

Circle the hat that matches the one Tutter is wearing.

Good catch, Treelo!

Help Ojo write in the numbers for a game of hopscotch.

Treelo blows lots of bubbles.

Color the smallest bubble orange.

Color the biggest bubble blue.

Look at all the pretty flowers! Color the biggest flower red.

Bear finds the cave he used to play in when he was a bear cub!

Ojo tries out Bear's old chair.

Bear remembers his old friends.

Snack time!

Draw a line to match Treelo, Tutter, and Pip and Pop with their favorite foods.

Ojo shares carrots with Christine Rabbit.

Buzzy the Bee brings Bear honey.

How many honey jars can you find in this picture?

Shadow shares a story with Bear.

When Bear feels an itchin', a scritchin', and a twitchin', it's time to cha-cha-cha.

Which picture of Bear is different?

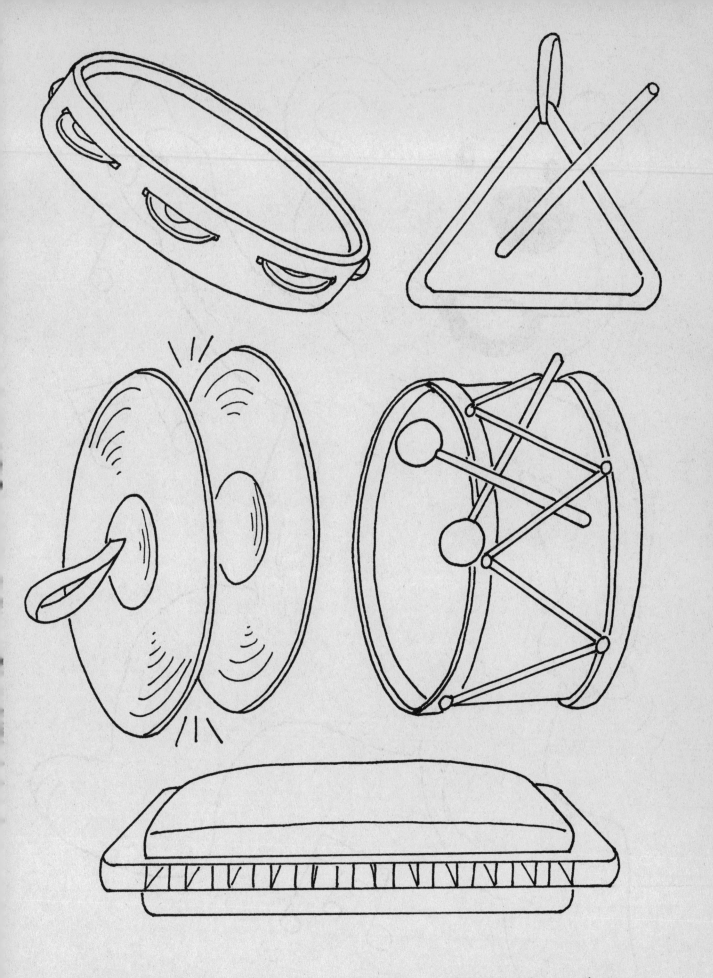

Draw a square around the instrument that Treelo is playing.

Who is dancing? To find out, use a blue crayon to color every space with the letter B. Use a pink crayon to color every space with the letter P.

Everyone likes a little quiet time after dancing.

What do you think Treelo is dreaming about? Draw a picture.

It's fun to look at photos.

Decorate the frame around Bear's picture.

Ojo loves this picture of her friend Ursa.

Look! Grandma Etta, Grandpa Otto, and Cousin Tally love clams, too!

MY FAMILY

Draw a picture of your family.

It's fun to make cards for friends.

Treelo loves feathers!

Pip and Pop make cards for their grandparents.

Make a card for someone you love. Have a grown-up help you cut it out.

TO:

- -

FROM:

Bear has lots of toys in his room.

Circle the two dinosaurs that are alike.

Howdy!

Can you help Bear find Tutter?

Color the triangles in this picture red.

How many things can you find in this picture that begin with the letter T?

Answer: Tuffer, Treelo, towels, toothpaste, toothbrush, tongue, tails.

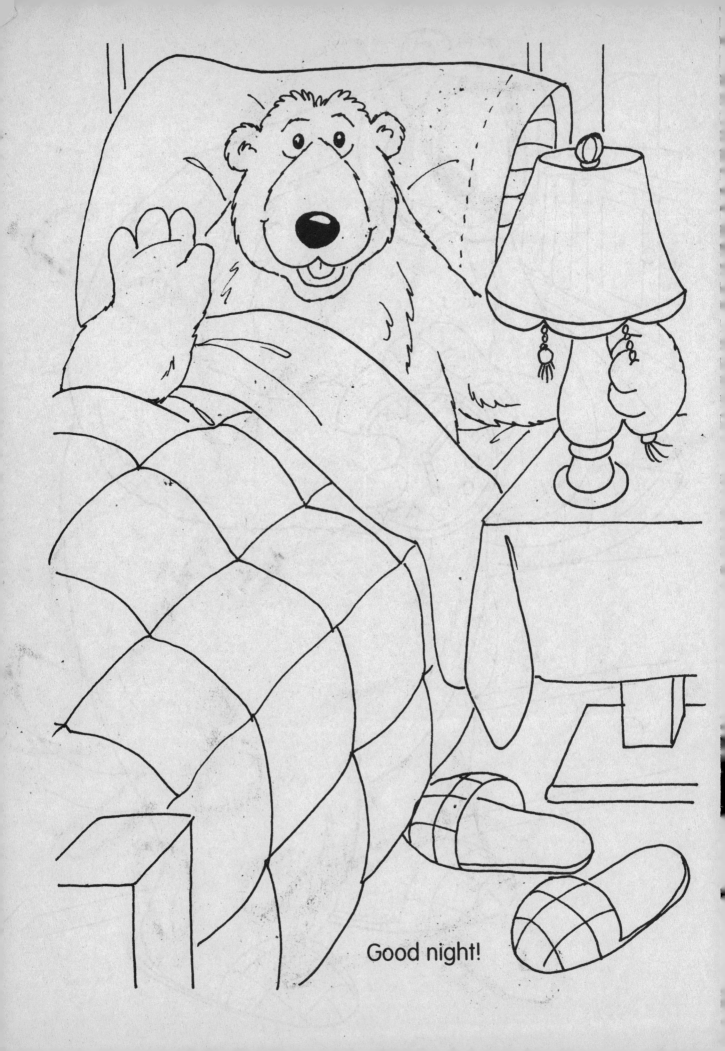

Good night!